Stepbrother Sabotage

Stepbrother Sabotage

by Sally Wittman
illustrated by Emily Arnold McCully

A TRUMPET CLUB SPECIAL EDITION

Published by The Trumpet Club
666 Fifth Avenue, New York, New York 10103

ISBN 0-440-84839-3

This edition published by arrangement with
HarperCollins Children's Books, a
division of HarperCollins Publishers
Printed in the United States of America
March 1992

1 3 5 7 9 10 8 6 4 2
OPM

For Joshua Zachary Wittman
with love

Stepbrother Sabotage

1

Here We Go Again!

A week before Jake comes to visit, we all—my mother, my stepfather, and I—start taking vitamins. Even the dog. If you knew Jake you'd understand why. The vitamins are for energy, because when Jake is around you get "worn down." At least that's what my mom says. I call the vitamins my "allergy" medicine. I am allergic to Jake.

Here's the deal: Jake is my stepbrother—he usually lives with his mom in Indianapolis, but he comes to visit during summer and winter vacations to see his father, who is my stepfather.

Jake's visits began two years ago when my mom and Jake's dad got married. That was a year and a half after Jake's mom and dad got divorced. And it was five years after my real father died. I like Fred (that's my stepfather's name). But having Jake come to stay twice a year is something I didn't count on. Like finding a cherry bomb in your Cheerios box.

I remember the first time I saw Jake. I told my mom I thought he looked like an angel—I mean, he had this straight, blond hair that hung down over these big, blue eyes. My mom laughed at that. "Angel?" she whispered in my ear. "I'm afraid, Joshua, that I've heard otherwise!" Unfortunately, she had heard right.

During Jake's visits my mom wants me to treat him like a real brother. "But he's not my brother," I tell her. "He's the creature from the black lagoon!" She doesn't find that funny. So I tell her he's really a "drifting conglomeration of lost cells from a biological warfare experiment." She doesn't laugh at that either. So I tell her I'll try to be nice to him. I get a smile for that.

The problem is Jake's behavior. Jake is eight going on nine, but he doesn't act like it. I know because I'm nine going on ten and I didn't act like that last year. In fact, nobody acts like Jake does. Last summer Jake ate a whole jar of pickles. I bet him he'd throw up, but he didn't. My mom says he's hyperactive. My stepfather says he's just a normal kid. All I know is when Jake comes to stay, my dog, Zephyr, hides under the dining-room table.

The last few days before Jake arrives my mom tries to begin several cheerful discussions with me about Jake's upcoming visit and how "we'll all try hard to make it go smoother than the last one, won't we, Joshua?" I groan, and my mom laughs and messes with my hair.

On the way to the airport to pick up Jake, my stepfather, Fred, whistles the whole way there. He must love Jake, though I can't see why. Maybe he started loving him when he was a little baby and now he can't stop. I mean, how can he love someone who wears his sweatshirt backward with the hood covering his face? I wonder if Fred loves me, too. I know my mom does, but she doesn't whistle about it. Maybe if I went away for a while, when I came back they'd appreciate me more.

Jake's plane taxis up the runway and guess who is the first one off. Jake, of course. When he blasts into the waiting room, it feels like we've been hit by a hailstorm. He talks nonstop all the way to our house, and then he races to the door and rings the doorbell ten times,

before the rest of us are even out of the car. Zephyr, who's been sleeping on the front porch, takes one look at Jake and runs so fast in the other direction that her spots turn into stripes.

Once we're inside, my stepfather takes Jake over to the sofa and has a talk with him about slowing down. It won't do any good. When Jake comes to stay, it's good-bye to relaxation.

I go to find my dog and have a little talk with her. I find her going through the neighbor's trash can and remember that in all the excitement I forgot to feed her before we left for the airport. "Come on, Zephyr," I say to her. "The whole family is going to try to make Jake's stay go smoothly. You've gotta do your part." She wags her tail and I scratch her under the chin. She gives me that suffering look that dogs get when people boss them around.

Back at the house, Jake is sitting on his dad's lap. They're laughing and talking. I look around for my mom, but she's busy in the kitchen.

Well, I promised I would be nice to Jake so I say, "C'mon, Jake! I'll help you unpack."

Jake charges up the stairs to my room. Then he immediately climbs up to my top bunk. He always sleeps there when he's visiting. Nobody ever asked me if I wanted to have Jake sleep in my top bunk—everybody just assumed that's where he would go. He usually turns it into a fort and I become the enemy and get bombarded. Last time he brought a squirt gun and attacked in the middle of the night, yelling "Geronimo!" He thought that was *sooooooo* funny.

Jake jumps down from the bunk and starts eating a bag of peanuts that he got on the airplane. I ask him how things have been in Indianapolis. "So-so," he says, munching and thumbing through the books on my bookshelf. I ask him how his mother is. "So-so," he says, while digging through my toy chest. I ask him how the school year went. "So-so," he says, checking out the top of my desk. I ask him how the baseball season went. "So-so," he says, nosing through my closet. He tries on my catcher's mitt and takes a few practice swings with my bat. Then, when he's run out of peanuts and run out of things to inspect, he climbs back onto the top bunk again. He takes a free shot toward my wastebasket with the peanut wrapper and misses. I pick it up. As I turn around I am blasted in the face by a cold stream of water, accompanied by fiendish laughter. How could I have once again become the target for his squirt gun?

After a while he says, "Are you glad to see me again?"

"So-so," I say without looking up.

2

A Lemony Sour Day

Coming downstairs the next morning, I am relieved to find that the living-room furniture is still in its proper place. One morning last Christmas, when Jake was visiting, we came downstairs to find that he had rearranged all the living-room furniture before the rest of us got up. The sofa was blocking the front door. Jake had decided we didn't need a front door—we could all go out the window!

This morning Jake is already up making breakfast. Last time he was here he made pancakes. His favorite trick was to send the pancakes flying onto the plates like Frisbees. But my mom caught one on the chin once, and that was the end of *that* trick. This morning Jake is making French toast. He is free-shooting the eggshells toward the disposal and Zephyr is leaping into the air trying to catch them before they land. It's a good thing my mom is still upstairs brushing her teeth. If she saw this scene, she'd croak!

When I go to get the orange juice, the cool air from the refrigerator gives me an idea. Then my mom walks in—just missing the eggshell scene.

"Okay if I have a lemonade stand, Mom?"

I guess I'm a little old for a lemonade stand, but my mom knows I'm trying to earn money for a new bike. "Sure," she says.

"I'm selling lemonade, too!" says Jake—just like that, without even asking.

My mom says I don't have to share my lemonade stand with Jake. "It would be *nice* if you would," she says, "but you don't have to." I'm not going to.

It takes me all morning to get ready. First I fill the ice trays, so the ice cubes will have time to get hard. Then I spend the rest of the morning making a sign and squeezing the lemons and mixing. Jake walks through the kitchen every few minutes and snoopervises everything. He even inspects the ice cubes in the freezer. He checks them several times.

"Cut it out, Jake!" I tell him, "They'll never get hard if you keep opening the freezer door."

"Just trying to be helpful," he says. "How much are you going to charge?"

"Twenty-five cents a glass," I say. "Why?"

"Just wondering," he says.

In the afternoon, when the temperature is soaring, I start carrying everything out to the front yard. A few little kids from the neighborhood hang around watching me set up my lemonade stand, but they don't have any money. So I keep busy arranging cups and napkins while I wait for customers.

Then, before you can say p-e-s-t, Jake sets up his own stand down the sidewalk a ways.

Jake doesn't have anything on the table to sell, but the kids with no money go down to have a look anyway. In a minute I hear them all laughing. So I go look, too. A sign in front of Jake's stand says I'LL SING YOU A SONG—20¢.

Boy, is that dumb! Who'd pay to hear Jake sing off-key?

Pretty soon two old ladies come walking down the street. I race back to my stand and wait for them. They're whispering to each other—probably discussing whether or not they should stop. I give them my best Boy Scout smile. They stop in front of my stand and each orders a glass of lemonade.

"What are you going to do with the money you earn today, young man?" one of the ladies asks.

I tell them I'm saving for a new bike. Then they walk down to Jake's stand. Both ladies giggle for a minute. Then they each plunk down a quarter. "Do you know 'In the Good Ol' Summertime'?" the first lady asks Jake.

"No," Jake says, "but that's okay—sing it for me and then I'll sing it back to you." Well, the old lady starts singing. It's the dumbest song, but finally she finishes singing and then Jake sings it back to her and she looks like she's going to cry. When he's finished, he sings another song for the second lady and she looks

like she's going to cry, too. I'm about to give them a napkin, when the first lady—the one who asked me what I was going to do with my money—asks Jake what *he's* going to do with *his* money. And he says—I can't believe this—he says in all seriousness that he's saving to buy his mom a gift with the money he earns! And both ladies croon and coo and tell him what a good boy he is and to KEEP THE CHANGE! Then both ladies fan themselves and sip at their lemonade.

Suddenly one of them spits out her lemonade and points to something in her glass. There is something in the ice cube, she says. Then the other lady starts poking at her lemonade and says there's something in hers, too. They both pour their lemonade into the gutter and glare at me as they walk away.

I investigate the other ice cubes in my lemonade pitcher. Almost every one has a bug in it. Then I remember Jake's trips to the refrigerator while I was making lemonade, and I get it: Jake was putting bugs into the ice cubes while he was pretending to see if they were hard! I've been sabotaged!

It's too late to make more ice cubes and nobody wants to buy warm lemonade, so I am forced to close down my lemonade stand. Since it's too hot to sit in the house, I sit on the front porch, drinking warm lemonade and listening to Jake sing to his customers in that squeaky voice of his. I can hear the coins jingle as he drops them into his money box.

Thinking about bugs has given me an idea of my own. When Jake isn't looking, I catch a spider in a jar. To be certain it isn't poisonous, I look it up in my spider book. That night, while Jake is brushing his teeth, I put it in the top bunk under his pillow.

3

Happy Birthday (sort of)

This morning Jake is fine. I'm covered with spider bites.

*   *   *

Sometimes I wish my real dad was still alive, so we wouldn't have to have Jake come to stay. But then I wouldn't have Fred, either, and he's pretty nice to me. Sometimes I wonder which one was nicer, my real dad or Fred? I don't remember my real dad very well—I was only two when he died. My only memory is of him throwing me into the air and catching me. That's all. Sometimes I have this dream that my dad is throwing me into the air and all of a sudden he throws me way up high and I'm scared and then he finally catches me, and I look but it isn't him. It's Fred....

Oh boy! I completely forgot—today is Fred's birthday, and I haven't gotten him a present yet. "Look, Mom," I tell her, "how can I buy Fred a present when I don't have any money? Jake earned money on his song stand, but he took away all the business from my lemonade stand. I'm completely broke."

My mom messes with my hair and says not to worry, she's got an idea. "Come into the kitchen," she says.

Two layers for a round layer cake are cooling on sheets of waxed paper on the kitchen counter. Beside them is a bowl of white frosting. Jake is sitting at the kitchen table dunking nacho-flavored taco chips into a glass of milk. Gross.

"How would you boys like to paint your own portraits on the two layers?

You could do them with frosting. I know Fred would love it!"

Jake and I both jump at the idea. My mom divides the frosting into two smaller bowls. She sets the food coloring and a bunch of cups and utensils between us. We each start with the face. We spread the frosting on with knives into face shapes. Then we do the eyes. Jake's are blue and mine are brown. We use the leftover brown to outline the noses and eyebrows. Then a little pink for the mouths. The hair is next. Jake makes his out of yellow frosting and he smooths it on with a knife. He even makes a part.

I start mixing more brown for my hair. I can't get the color right so I mix in a little cocoa. I sample it with my finger —it's not bad. "What should I do about my curls?" I ask my mom. She hands me the garlic press. Great! I put some brown frosting in the garlic press and squeeze. Long skinny brown strands ooze from the holes and I dangle them over my portrait until they touch down, just above the ear. Then I keep reloading and dangling more strands until I have formed a head of hair that looks just like mine.

My mom says she's really proud of both of us and that we both show a great deal of artistic talent. As she's saying it, she leans over the table and puts her arms around both of us. Jake squirms away. I don't think he likes my mom to touch him. It's funny—Jake spends all his time trying to get attention, but when you act nice to him, he looks like he doesn't want you to.

Personally, I think my picture is better than Jake's, but we'll see what Fred thinks. My mom puts the cakes up in a cupboard so he won't see them right away.

When Fred gets home from work we have fried chicken for dinner—it's his favorite. After we're finished he drives Jake and me down to pick out some videos. He says it's our choice. We tell him it's *his* choice, it's *his* birthday. But he insists that we choose—that's the way Fred is. Since Fred insists that we choose, I choose a Berkeley Boys mystery and Jake picks some monster movie.

At home, my mom has already set the table for dessert. "Jake, would you like to go first and bring out your cake?" she says. Jake is in there a long time. He comes out carrying a tall cake. With a sudden, sinking feeling I realize why it's so tall—Jake has put his layer on top of my layer. My face is now stuck to the underside of Jake's layer. That unbelievable oozing blob of a slimy stepbrother of mine has sabotaged me once again!

24

My mom motions to me not to say anything. I know what she's thinking. She's trying to figure out how to show my portrait to Fred without causing a scene and ruining his birthday. When Fred stops talking, my mom quietly takes the knife and begins to separate the two layers. Finally, she lifts the top layer and shifts it to another plate. We pick at the crumbs covering my face. My curly hair has been flattened, but with a little crumb dusting you can begin to see that it's a picture of someone, someone vaguely familiar.

Jake is starting to get up from the table. Fred doesn't get it at first, but then he begins to realize what's happened.

"Wait a minute, Jake," he says. "Sit down and have your cake. We'll discuss this later." Then he turns to me. He looks me straight in the eyes and says in the nicest voice, "You must have put a lot of work into that picture, Joshua, and I really appreciate it." He reaches over and puts his hand on my shoulder. That takes some of the sting away from what Jake has done.

There's an awkward silence and then everyone has two slices of cake, one from Jake's and one from mine. Finally, we break the silence by laughing over the way the pictures get divided. I get my left eye and Jake's right ear. Fred says that they're the best birthday cakes he's ever tasted. Fred's pretty nice. He can't help it that his son is a dingbat.

After dessert we watch the videos and everybody pretends to forget about what Jake has done. Then, when it's time to go upstairs, I hear Fred ask Jake to stay behind.

Later, when the lights are out, I can hear Jake sniffing in the top bunk. I wonder if he's crying. The thought of him crying makes me feel awful. I don't know why I should feel sorry for him, after all the stuff he's done to me. I mean, I should feel mad, shouldn't I? So will someone please tell me why, when Jake sniffs and sounds like he's crying, I—of all people—get a stomachache?

4

Ignoring Jake

Right now I'm sitting on the sofa in my pajamas, watching Jake outside practicing with my pogo stick. Jake likes to do everything big. He once drew a hopscotch board on the sidewalk that was seven blocks long. Another time he practiced with a Hula Hoop until he could twirl it four hundred times. Now he's yelling at me that he just jumped on the pogo stick six hundred and forty-six times. It seems like he wants everything he does to go into the *Guinness Book of Records*. I decide to call up my best friend, Bobby, to see if he wants to do something. First thing he says is "Wait a minute—this is August, isn't it?"

"Uh-huh," I say, knowing what comes next.

"Your stepbrother, Jake, is visiting, isn't he?"

"Yeah," I say, knowing what comes after that, too.

"Call me back in September," he says, "after Jake goes home."

I guess it's understandable. Last summer when Jake was here, we visited Bobby. Bobby and I were downstairs watching T.V. and Jake was upstairs supposedly playing some video game. Then I guess Jake got lonely and decided to make some new friends. He used Bobby's phone to direct-dial all over the world. The phone bill was two feet long!

It's the same with everyone I call. They've all got their reasons for not wanting to see Jake.

I'm sitting on the sofa daydreaming about this when I am startled back to reality by a voice calling me. It's my mom. She and Jake are both standing there. She has to go to the doctor. Just a checkup, she says, and I can go with her. I jump at the chance to get out of the house. Unfortunately, so does Jake.

My mom tells us to wait for her in the supermarket next to the doctor's office. She says we can take her grocery list and do some of the shopping for her. She says if Jake and I keep busy and ignore each other, we'll get along better. Maybe she's right.

When we get to the supermarket I tell Jake to go find the pinto beans while I get the flour, then to meet me in the frozen food section. At the end of the flour aisle there is a large display of cheddar cheese spread. A young man is spreading it onto crackers and handing

them out. Behind him is a large box containing entries to a contest. The young man smiles at me and nods toward the box. "To enter, you have to write a jingle about cheddar cheese spread," he says. "The first prize is a blue Olympus racing bike. Today is the last day to enter and the winner will be notified tonight."

I'd give anything to win that bike! As soon as we get home I ride my old bike to the bike store. My old bike is too small and it's a little kid's style, but my mom said I can't get a new one before Christmas. I'll die of embarrassment before Christmas.

The salesman at the bike store says that the Olympus is the best racing bike they sell. I tell him about the contest at the supermarket. He smiles and says, "Well, if you don't win the contest and you've got four hundred dollars to spend, come back and see me and I'll sell you one."

"I've already got more money saved than he has!" a familiar voice behind me pipes up. It's Jake. He has followed me to the bike store.

I could explain to the salesman that it's because Jake lies to old ladies and wrecks other people's lemonade stands that he's able to save so much money. But he wouldn't believe me anyway.

When we get home, I try again to ignore Jake. I spend the rest of the afternoon writing jingles. My second-best jingle goes like this:

Cheddar cheese is yummy
Cheddar cheese is nice
Cheddar cheese will really
Give your life some spice.

But my real winner is this one:

Say cheese for the camera
Say cheese when you smile
Say cheddar cheese in Egypt
When you're floating down the Nile.

I write each jingle, in my neatest handwriting, on a sheet of my mom's blue stationery (blue—to match the bike, get it?). Then I tell my mom I'm going back to the supermarket to deliver my entries. I've just got to win!

Jake-the-pest follows me to the store. "This contest is so stupid," he says, as I push my entries into the box.

After dinner I sit by the phone, waiting. Around seven o'clock the phone rings. It's for Jake....

Jake has won second prize in the jingle contest! And I never even saw him enter! His prize is two tickets to Water World. His entry was really dumb. It went:

I'd cheddar be dead
than give up your spread!

The man from the supermarket says it was "daring and original."

Then the man asks to speak to me. As I take the receiver I whisper to Jake, "Maybe I'll give you my old bike."

"Congratulations!" the man says. "You have won honorable mention! The prize is two cases of Cheery Cheddar Cheese Spread!" I hang up the phone before I begin to scream.

"I HATE CHEDDAR CHEESE SPREAD! CHEDDAR CHEESE SPREAD MAKES ME WANT TO BARF!"

"It's not bad on celery," Jake says.

At least he didn't win the bike.

5

A Scrambled-Eggs and Wild-Cherry Day

My mom doesn't feel like cooking breakfast this morning, and though nobody says so, I think everyone is getting tired of Jake's French toast. So today we're going out for breakfast. I wonder if my parents realize what they're doing. "You know Jake never behaves in public places," I remind my mom.

"Well then, it's time for him to learn," she says, giving me a wink. I'm not sure what that's supposed to mean.

At the restaurant, my mom isn't feeling well and excuses herself to go to the bathroom. Fred orders for both of them and follows her. He calls over his shoulder to the waitress, "The boys can have whatever they want, within reason." I hate it when he calls us "the boys," as if Jake is my real brother or something.

The waitress is very big and very tough looking. I mean she's polite and stuff but she looks like the kind of person you wouldn't want to fiddle with. She takes my order first. I order bacon and eggs and orange juice. Then she turns to Jake. He doesn't say anything.

"And you?" says the waitress, staring at Jake with eyes like two laser beams. "What'll you have?"

Jake has been watching her. I can tell he's trying to think of something to get her goat.

"I'll have the cheese and sausage omelette…" Jake says, and the waitress writes it down. Then he continues, "…but without the cheese and without the sausage." She looks at him over her glasses.

"Something to drink?" she says.

"Yeah," he says, "I'll have hot chocolate…"

She writes again.

"…but cold instead of hot and without the chocolate, and hold the whipped cream."

She doesn't look up this time. Just taps her pencil on her order pad. "Anything else?"

"Cinnamon toast…" he says innocently.

But before he can finish, she says, "Wait—let me guess. You want me to hold the cinnamon?"

Jake looks at her with a straight face and says, "And substitute honey."

The woman writes for a minute; then with a smile that could crack an axle, she says in a steely voice, "We aim to please." Then she turns and walks away.

When our parents get back to the table, Jake has just finished pouring half the salt from the saltshaker into the sugar bowl.

"Everything okay?" my stepfather asks.

I think about telling on Jake but then the food comes and everyone's busy with that. We get served in the same order as we ordered, which means Jake is last.

"Scrambled eggs, toast and milk," says the waitress, placing the dishes before Jake. "Anything else?" Her eyes lock him in a stare that would make a Bengal tiger curl up and suck on its tail.

"No thanks," Jake says sweetly.

When we leave the restaurant Jake lags behind for a minute. I see him slip a piece of paper under his plate.

"What did you write?" I ask on the way to the car, but Jake won't tell me.

As we drive away I see the waitress

run out on the sidewalk waving her fist at Jake. I'm afraid for a minute that she's going to run after us—and she could probably catch us, too. But finally she shrugs and turns around and goes back toward the restaurant. Our parents didn't see a thing. Jake makes another clean getaway. I don't know how he does it. He finally told me what it was that he wrote. He told the waitress that if she wanted the tip his dad had left her, she would find it in the bottom of the orange juice glass.

"The day is still beginning," says Fred. "How about a trip to the history museum, everybody?"

With Jake? Is he kidding? We'd have to be crazy to go to the history museum with Jake. He already made trouble at the restaurant, even if Fred didn't see. Jake could destroy the entire history of the human race before lunchtime. But

I'm not saying anything. Nobody listens to me anyway.

At the museum Jake and I race up the large staircase and wait on the porch behind the marble columns for my mom and Fred. My mom is walking slowly. She still isn't feeling well. I bet I could make her feel a whole lot worse if I told her what really went on at the restaurant.

Charley, the guard in the museum, is my friend. We usually come here in the winter and he always remembers me and gives me a wild-cherry Lifesaver.

"How ya doin', ol' buddy?" says Charley.

"Not bad."

"Who's this you got with you?"

"This is my stepbrother, Jake."

"How do, Jake. You boys going up to check out the armor?"

"You bet." Charley knows it's always the first place I head for. Before we take off he gives us each a Lifesaver. I can't believe how wild cherry always tastes exactly the same, summer or winter, indoors or out.

We race upstairs and look at the armor. This is a small museum so there are only two suits of armor. First we look at the Norman suit and then we look at the German one.

"I wonder how they went to the bathroom in those things," Jake says.

"Maybe they didn't. I mean maybe they didn't eat or drink anything before they went to battle so they didn't have to go."

But Jake has got me curious and I'm investigating the armor a little more closely when he says, "Hey, check this out."

I turn around and just about go through the roof—Jake has taken the armor helmet off one of the knight man nequins and has put it on his own head.

"On guard!" he says, waving his arm like an imaginary sword.

"Jake! Get that off before someone catches you." I reach for him, but he jumps away. So I ignore him and go back to what I was doing.

"Here," he says, "hold this while I try to get the sword loose." The next thing I know I am looking through iron mesh and tiny eye spaces. Jake has plopped the helmet on my head. I start to pull it off but it feels so solid that I can't help spending just a minute imagining that I'm a knight riding on a large, white horse. I can almost hear the hoof-beats....Uh-oh! Those aren't hoofbeats —they're footsteps!

"Hey, Jake! Quick, help me off with this." I can't get the helmet off. I turn around, but Jake hears the footsteps, too, and returns the sword to its proper

place. "Jake, if I get caught with this on my head, I'll have to go to jail and then I won't ever save enough money to buy an Olympus. Of course, if I went to jail I wouldn't get to ride it anyway. Hey Jake, aren't you going to help me?"

But Jake has run into the next room. I run after him. We're in the antique-furniture room. With a lurch in my stomach, I remember that this room is a dead end. I don't see Jake anywhere. He must be hiding. I look for a place to hide, too. I squeeze into the cabinet of a large grandfather clock. My heart is pounding and my breath is steaming up the inside of the helmet. In a second I hear Charley's voice.

"Fond of antique furniture, are you?" Charley says. I wonder if he's talking to Jake or to me. My knees are shaking like twin earthquakes.

I hear Charley's voice right above me.

"Time to set this ol' clock," he says. "It's always losing time."

I hear a noise above me, like a window opening or something. Then I hear a clicking noise.

Suddenly the clock starts to play a little melody, except it's a pretty big melody when you're inside where the melody's coming from. Then a huge clang echoes inside the helmet and rings in my ears. I can't cover my ears because the helmet is in the way. Before the first one has stopped echoing there is another. On the third clang I burst out of the clock and run right into someone's arms. The clock noise is almost drowned out by Charley's laughter. He wiggles the helmet off my head. Then I can see—it isn't just Charley laughing, it's Jake, too. Jake is standing there laughing and he's the one who put the helmet on my head in the first place.

That's it! This time I'm telling on him!

"He did it!" I point to Jake. Jake turns and runs.

"Sure doesn't look like it!" says Charley, between laughs. "I mean you been caught with what they call 'smoking-gun evidence.'" He looks after Jake and shakes his head. Then he turns back to me and I'm still standing there. "But you got a clean record," he says. "And that counts for a lot."

I look at the floor. Maybe it's better not to say anything at all. Charley points his Lifesaver pack in my direction. I take one without looking up.

"Take one for your brother, too," says Charley, pushing the roll at me again. I take another. I pop mine into my mouth. I can't help noticing that wild cherry still tastes the same, even when you've just been caught red-handed, and you weren't even guilty.

I sneak a look at Charley. He's smiling. "Promise you won't do it again?" he says in a voice that tells me he already knows my answer.

"I promise."

"Then run along." I don't explain to Charley that the reason I can be certain I won't do it again is that I am moving to Tibet tomorrow.

I walk downstairs slowly. My ears are still ringing. I find Jake with our parents in the historic paintings section. When our parents aren't looking, Jake points his finger at me and laughs silently. I stick the Lifesaver that was supposed to be for Jake on the end of my tongue and waggle it at him. "Hey, no fair. I get one!" says Jake.

"Sorry," I say. "Last one. Going, going, gone!" *Crunch. Crunch.* I slurp more than necessary as the last bits melt in my mouth.

6

A Rare and Mysterious Condition

Something is going on around here. My mom has been whispering a lot to my stepfather. And there have been a lot of phone calls. I answer the phone whenever I can, but my mom always gets there first.

I try to listen in. But my mom says, "I've got it already, dear, you can hang up now."

Today Dr. Schmidt's office called again. Someone must be sick. I watch everyone carefully. My mom looks okay. Fred looks okay. Jake looks terrible. But then Jake always looks terrible. To me, anyway.

Is it possible that someone in our family could be ill and not know it—like me, for example? I go to the library and check out a book on diseases. It's filled with pictures of people with big lumps and people covered with red sores and people with hair growing everywhere. It gives me the creeps to look at these pictures. But I look anyway. I spend the day reading.

"What're you doing?" Jake asks.

"Nothing," I tell him. But later I come back from the bathroom and find him on the rug, turning the pages of the book on diseases.

"WOW! This is gross!" he says, pointing to a picture of a woman whose nostrils look like two cannonballs hit her in the face. "Look at that!" he says, pointing to another one of a man with warts all over his body. I know I'll never get Jake away from that book now, so I settle down on the rug beside him and we flip through the pages together. The pictures are so fascinating that I almost forget Jake is Jake. I think he forgets I'm me, too.

Later, we decide to examine each other for signs of disease. Jake sits on the bunk while I listen to him breathe. I check his skin. I smell his breath. I examine his fingernails and toenails. I decide that either he is normal or he has something so rare that it won't be found in the neighborhood library. I reluctantly inform him that he is normal.

Then it's Jake's turn to examine me. He smells my breath. "Gross—peanut butter!" he says. He examines my fingernails and toenails. "If you don't clip your toenails pretty soon, they're going to curl under in circles," he warns me. Then he checks my skin.

"Hold up your arms, Joshua!" he says as he pulls up my T-shirt. He has it up

almost over my head, and he starts to tickle me. I can't defend myself with my shirt blocking my arms. But once I get it down, I whap him with my pillow. Then he grabs his pillow and we have an all-out pillow fight. We're laughing and screaming. Nobody even comes to check. I guess they figure if we're laughing we can't be fighting. And we're not!

The next day my mom says I look a little pale and asks if I feel all right. I tell her I'm just tired, but I don't tell her it's because I was up most of the night reading about rare diseases with Jake. She says she's tired, too, and lies down on the sofa.

Jake will be going back to his mom's the day after tomorrow. He is very quiet today. It's funny—yesterday we actually had fun together, but today he's hardly talking to me. I guess he's sad about leaving his dad. I wonder if I'll miss Jake when he goes back to Indianapolis.

I go up to my room. Jake is lying on his back in the top bunk. His arms are crossed over his chest like a corpse. A thought pops into my mind. I wonder if I'd miss him if he died.

"Jake," I say, "if you died, where would you want to be buried?"

"I don't want to be buried," he says slowly, without opening his eyes.

"You mean you want to be cremated?"

"No," says Jake. "I've got it all figured out. I want to be ground up and put into one of those soft-serve chocolate ice cream machines."

"Jake! Are you serious?"

He's sitting up now and laughing. "Sure! With fudge sauce and nuts would be the best way. But just plain would probably be okay, too."

Ugh! I feel sick all day. When it's time for dinner, I can only pick at the food on my plate. And on top of that, guess what we have for dessert. Chocolate ice cream.

"No thanks," I say, excusing myself from the table. As I leave the kitchen I hear Jake asking if he can have my ice cream, too. I bet he knew about the ice cream all the time.

After dinner our parents say that they would like to speak to us in the living room.

"Boys…" Fred clears his throat. "We have something to tell you."

What's going on? This sounds like a line from the movies. I look at Jake. He's cracking his knuckles.

Fred smiles. "Your mom and I are expecting a baby."

Nobody says anything. Dead silence.

My mom looks puzzled. "Well, what do you think about the baby?"

I look over at Jake. "Yuck!" he says, and runs upstairs.

"Ditto!" I say, and go sit on the front porch.

I walk around for a while and then I go back into the house. My parents are in the kitchen. I can hear Fred's voice saying, "It will take a while for the boys to get used to the idea."

Up in my room I find Jake sitting on the floor beside his open suitcase. I spot my prize yo-yo stuck in between his socks.

"Hey, who said you could have that?" I grab it back.

When Jake looks up, he is so sad I can hardly believe it. Right away, I get that achy feeling in the pit of my stomach. I toss the yo-yo back to him. "Here, keep it," I say. "I don't need it after all."

I flop down on my bunk. "Hey, Jake, what do you think we ought to do about the baby?"

"Call the National Guard," says Jake,

standing up. And without a word, he heads downstairs.

In about five minutes I hear a siren. It gets louder and louder. There is an ambulance parked in front of our house. I run downstairs to check it out.

Jake really did call the National Guard. He says it was because their ad says WE'RE ALWAYS THERE WHEN YOU NEED HELP. So Jake looked up the number and dialed it and said, "My stepmom's having a baby—so what are you going to do about it?"

The man asked for Jake's address and then he said, "Don't worry, son, help is on the way."

My mom had to explain to the ambulance people that there was a misunderstanding—the baby wasn't due for months.

Jake is taking this baby news pretty hard. I guess he doesn't like the idea of having another brother or sister when he doesn't get along with the one he's already got. I understand exactly how he feels.

At night I hear Jake sniffing in his bunk again. This time I decide to find out what's happening. "Hey, Jake, are you crying or what?"

A blast of cold water on my head is all I get for an answer. I jump out of bed, ready to strangle Jake. But then—wonder of wonders—he says he's sorry. And I hear myself saying that it's okay. Then I crawl back under the covers and lie there thinking about Jake and me and everything.

7

A New Plan

There's something buzzing outside! It must be Mr. Gladstone mowing his lawn. Who else would be up at six in the morning?

After a while I hear a lot of commotion outside. I look out the window. What I heard earlier wasn't Mr. Gladstone mowing his lawn. It was Jake shearing the hedge into strange shapes. I run downstairs to see.

It was a crude job, but I can make out the letters of his name. Jake is leaving today, but his name will remain with us for months, until the hedge starts to grow again in the spring.

"I think Jake is trying to tell us not to forget him," I say to my mom.

"I think you're right," my mom says.

Jake looks scared—he thinks he's in trouble. But my mom surprises him. She goes over and gives him a big hug. At first Jake gets an expression on his face like he's being strangled by a boa constrictor. Then he does an amazing thing—for Jake. He hugs her back.

Jake is quiet on the way to the airport. Just before he leaves he tells me he has a secret plan this trip for getting more bags of peanuts on the airplane.

"They only give out one bag per person," I tell him. "Two, if you tell them you're starving and about to die from malnutrition."

When Jake boards the plane I see him whisper something to the flight attendant. Then he waves from the window. He is grinning and holding at least *six*

bags of peanuts!

Nobody talks on the way back from the airport. It's always that way when Jake leaves. Nobody talks during dinner, either. My stomach growls and nobody laughs the way they usually do. Fred looks glum and my mom keeps watching him. I feel funny, too—kind of empty or something.

After dinner my mom says, "We could make some popcorn and watch an old movie on T.V."

I fake a yawn and say, "No, I guess I'll go read for a while and get to bed early." When I open the door to my room, a water trap spills right on top of my head—a direct hit. One last prank by Jake.

I go to sit on my bunk. Then I climb up to Jake's bunk—correction—*my* bunk. I'm sitting there thinking how peaceful it will be with Jake gone when I remember something. I wonder if Jake forgot to take his squirt gun. I reach under the pillow. The squirt gun isn't there, but there is something else—an envelope. It's a letter to Jake from his mom.

I know that reading someone else's mail is wrong, but drops of water are still running down the back of my neck from Jake's water trap. I can almost hear my mom's voice saying, "Two wrongs don't make a right," as I pull the letter out of the envelope.

Dearest Jake,

I'm sorry things have been hard for you. I know how hard it is to share a room with your stepbrother. It is always hard to live in the same house with someone when you feel they don't like you. Try to be kind to Joshua: I'm sure it is awkward for him, too. And remember, things

could change for the better.

Thank you so much for the lovely birthday present. I know you are homesick and I miss you terribly, too, but the cologne you sent me is lovely and every time I wear it I'll think of you. How clever of you to think of singing songs to earn the money for it! Remember to brush your teeth and wear your headgear.

I love you,

Mommie

So Jake really did spend his money on a gift for his mom. He never talks about his mom. I didn't know he was homesick, either.

After rereading the letter from Jake's mom a couple of times, I get a weird idea. I sit down and write Jake a letter. It's the first time I've ever written him.

I tell him:

We're in this together. If you think things were tough around here before, just wait till the baby comes! You know what I think? We should both write to the Buddhist monastery in Tibet. Monks believe in brotherhood. Maybe they would agree to accept us if we come together.

I got a letter from Jake today. It's the first time he's ever written me. I take it to my room and climb up into my top bunk to read it. It says:

Tibet is too far away. How about going to Water World together instead? I've got two tickets, remember?

Then he wrote at the bottom of the page:

P.S. Did you find the surprise I left? Ha-ha!

P.S. #2 Babies make me want to barf!

P.S. #3 I'll bring you some peanuts next time I come—if you're lucky.

I can almost see the way Jake looked when he wrote those last lines—his funny, evil smile and his croaking-frog laugh.

Laughing out loud at the thought of him, I fold Jake's letter and put it back in its envelope. Then I jump down to the floor and go to my desk. I flip the calendar to December. I stand there for a minute, debating. Then I circle the date when Jake will come to stay.

Jake and I have until Christmas to decide what we're going to do about the coming baby. With two great minds working together, I'm sure we can come up with something.